How Sleep Found Tabitha

How Sleep Found Tabitha

by Maggie deVries
illustrated by Sheena Lott

Sweet dreams!
Maggie de Vries

Orca Book Publishers

Sleep would not come to Tabitha.
Her eyes, round as headlights, roamed the room.

On the rocking chair she saw the bedtime story Gram had read earlier. She saw her clothes in a heap on the teddy-bear rug. She saw the soft glow of her night light and the golden stripe shining through the gap around her door. She saw dim shadows all about the room.

Nowhere could she see sleep.

But she could hear sleep calling from far and wide.
"Come sleep with me in the deep blue sea," sang the whale.

Tabitha didn't have a breathing hole in her back,
so she stayed right where she was.

"Sleep high up here, where the sky is clear," cried the eagle. Tabitha thought she might tumble out of the nest once she fell asleep, so she snuggled down deeper in her bed.

"Come muddily rest; the sludge is the best," croaked the frog.
The mud would get awfully cold in the night, thought Tabitha,
and she listened some more.

"Sleep up on all fours and dream out of doors," called the horse.

Tabitha got onto all fours under her covers. She could tell it wouldn't be comfortable for long, so she flopped down as hard as she could.

"Come slither to sleep where it's dark and it's deep," whispered the snake.

Tabitha slithered out of bed and onto the rug. But the only dark, deep place in her house was the basement, and she wasn't going there, so she slithered right back up again.

"We'll romp and we'll play. We'll sleep in sea spray," barked the seal.

Tabitha romped. Tabitha played. But without a seal's thick blubber she couldn't sleep on sharp rocks drenched in salty water, so she slipped back under the warm, dry covers.

"Below ground is the place to build a sleep space,"
murmured the rabbit.

A cave could be cozy, Tabitha thought, and she made one in the blankets. Dirt might fall in her eyes and mouth, she realized, so she stuck her head out and listened for another voice.

But this time no voice called to Tabitha.

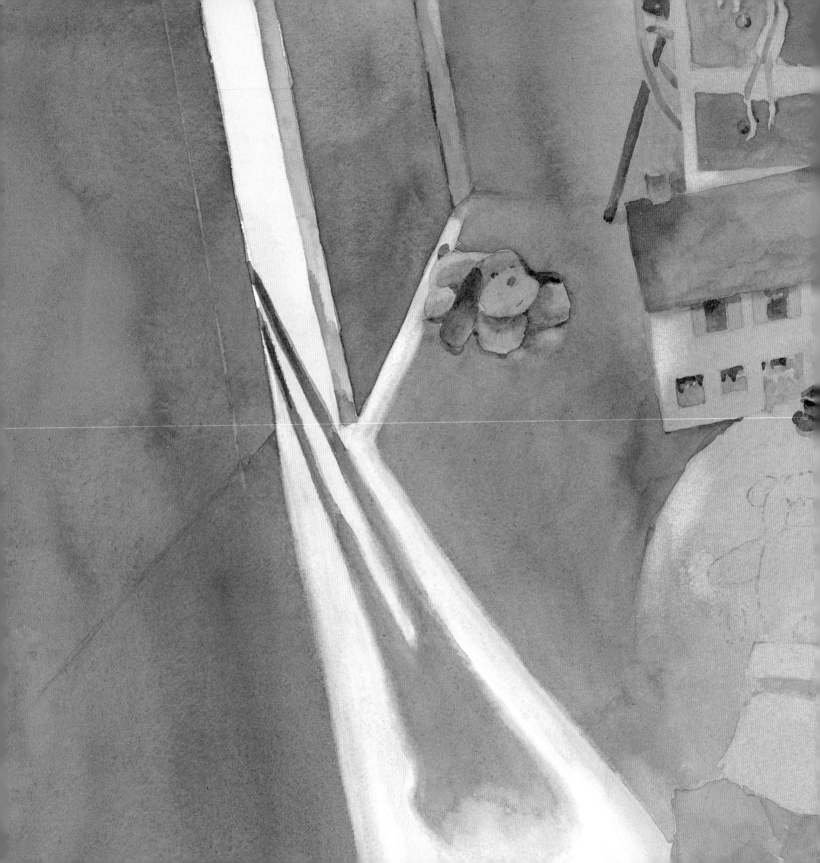

This time sleep came creeping from far and wide.
He slipped through the gap of her very own door. And padded
across her very own floor and leaped onto her very own bed.

"I'll curl up with you. We'll sleep here, we two," purred the soft, grey cat as he wiggled his way deep down under the covers.

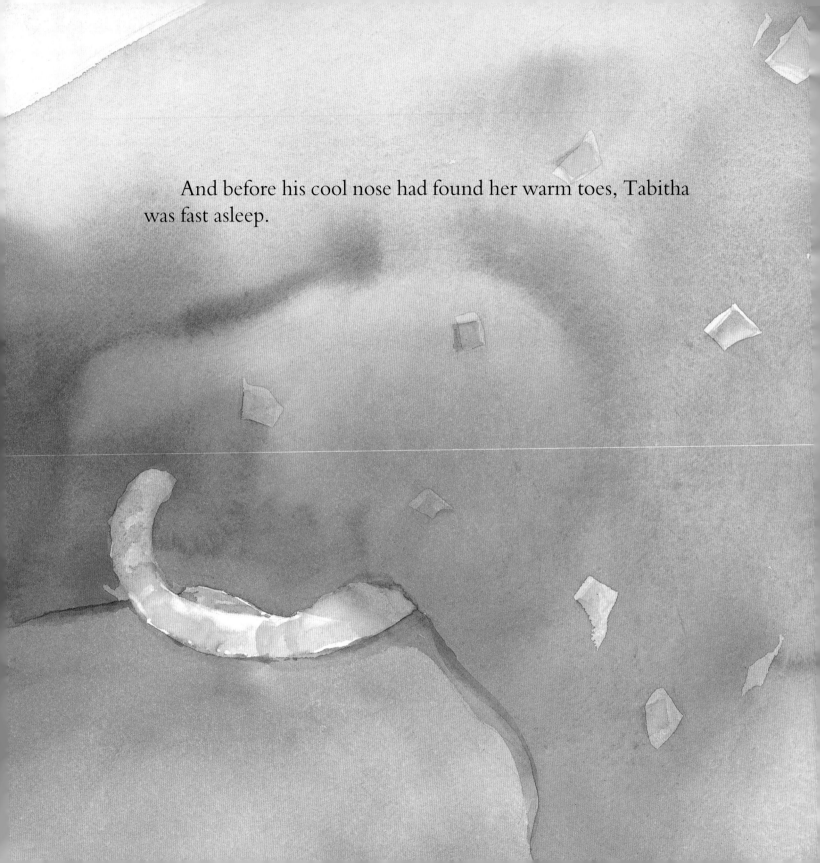

And before his cool nose had found her warm toes, Tabitha was fast asleep.

National Library of Canada Cataloguing in Publication Data
De Vries, Maggie.

How sleep found Tabitha

ISBN 1-55143-193-9

I. Lott, Sheena, 1950- II. Title.

PS857.E895H68 2002 jC813'.54 C2001-911541-5

PZ7.D515Ho 2002

First published in the United States, 2002

Library of Congress Catalog Card Number: 2001097710

Orca Book Publishers gratefully acknowledges the support of our publishing programs provided by the following agencies: the Department of Canadian Heritage, The Canada Council for the Arts, and the British Columbia Arts Council.

Design by Christine Toller
Printed and bound in Hong Kong

Orca Book Publishers
PO Box 5626, Station B
Victoria, BC Canada
V8R 6S4

Orca Book Publishers
PO Box 468
Custer, WA   USA
98240-0468

04 03 02 • 5 4 3 2 1

The Tzar's Bird

Ann Tompert · Illustrated by Robert Rayevsky

Macmillan Publishing Company   New York
Collier Macmillan Publishers   London

Macmillan Publishing Company

866 Third Avenue, New York, NY 10022

Collier Macmillan Canada, Inc.

Printed and bound in Hong Kong   First American Edition

10   9   8   7   6   5   4   3   2   1

The text of this book is set in 16 point Perpetua.

The illustrations are rendered in pen-and-ink, watercolor and acrylic.

Library of Congress Cataloging-in-Publication Data

Tompert, Ann. The Tzar's bird/Ann Tompert;

illustrated by Robert Rayevsky. —

1st American ed.   p.   cm.

Summary: A tzar's fear of going to the edge of the

world grows when Baba Yaga threatens him, but in time

he learns that fear of the unknown is a senseless fear.

ISBN 0-02-789401-0

1. Baba Yaga (Legendary character) — Juvenile fiction.

[1. Baba Yaga (Legendary character) — Fiction.

2. Soviet Union — Fiction.   3. Fear — Fiction.

4. Fairy tales.]   I. Rayevsky, Robert, ill.   II. Title.

PZ8.T537Tz   1990   [E] — dc19

89-31376   CIP   AC

To Agnes

Many years ago, when Grand Prince Yaroslav was crowned tzar of a small province in a far corner of Russia, he celebrated by giving a magnificent banquet for all the important people under his rule. In the midst of the feasting and merrymaking, loud cackling laughter reverberated throughout the palace.

"It's Baba Yaga!" someone cried.

Terrified screams filled the air. Several people fainted, and the rest shrank to the corners of the hall. But Yaroslav stood firm.

In sailed the bony-legged witch, Baba Yaga, propelling her mortar with a pestle and sweeping away her tracks with a broom.

"Welcome, grandmother," said Yaroslav, bowing and smiling.

"Welcome!" shouted Baba Yaga. "How welcome am I? Did you think me important enough to invite me to your coronation? No! Never mind. I have a gift for you, nonetheless." And she thrust a glittering cage into Yaroslav's hands.

A gasp of astonishment swept through the crowd, for in the cage was a firebird.

"Heed my words," cried Baba Yaga. "If any harm should come to this firebird or if it should become unhappy, you shall go to the Outermost Edge of the World."

With that she sailed out the way she had come in, her shrill cackle rattling the very windows of the palace.

Now, no one had ever been there, but everyone believed that the Outermost Edge of the World was dark and dank and dismal and filled with loathsome, hideous creatures. Yaroslav was brave of heart, but fear seized him when he thought of that place.

How can I keep the firebird safe and happy? he wondered.

Yaroslav asked his Royal Advisers for help.

The Court Architect said, "A happy bird likes to spread its wings." And Yaroslav gave the firebird a little park enclosed in a cage of glass.

The Court Baker said, "If you feed the firebird little honey cakes, it will never wish to leave you." And the tzar ordered him to have an ample supply always available.

Because the Court Minstrel told Yaroslav that sweet music made all creatures content, the tzar gathered the best musicians in the kingdom to stroll about and serenade the firebird.

And when the Court General said, "Your enemies may try to
harm the firebird to get rid of you," Yaroslav ordered two dozen
and three soldiers stationed around the cage.

When winter came, the tzar installed blue-and-white-tiled stoves so that the firebird enjoyed everlasting summer. And he hung lanterns to chase away the early evening darkness.

Although he had done everything he could to safeguard and please the firebird, Yaroslav was still concerned that some evil would befall it. In the end he decided that it would be best if he lived with the firebird — alone. He turned over the affairs of his

country to his ministers, built a little house for himself in the firebird's park, and sent everyone away, including the musicians and soldiers. He even refused to let his queen visit him.

"I must devote my every moment to the firebird," he said when she protested. And Yaroslav did faithfully attend to the needs of the firebird, singing to it every day and baking the little honey cakes it loved so well.

One year passed, two years passed, and then two more. A tangled jungle of bushes and vines and trees hugged the caged park. Yaroslav forgot his fear of the Outermost Edge of the World. And with his loss of fear he became more careless each day, until finally he stopped making the little honey cakes. The firebird's eyes lost their sparkle and its feathers grew dull, but Yaroslav did not notice.

Then one day, when the firebird was sitting in its favorite tree with its tail drooping, Baba Yaga soared out of the sky in her mortar. She crashed through the ceiling of the cage, filling the air with a shower of splintered glass. "Did you think you could escape the Outermost Edge of the World forever?" she shrieked. And picking up the firebird, she sailed out through the hole she had made in the cage.

"Come back! Come back!" cried Yaroslav, running to the door of the cage. "Give me my firebird."

He stepped out into the thick tangle of vines and bushes and trees. The air echoed with Baba Yaga's wild cackle. "Outermost Edge of the World! Outermost Edge of the World!"

Without stopping to think, Yaroslav began to rip his way through the green wall. Thorn bushes tore his hands and face and clothes. Vines and roots tripped him. Insects swarmed about and bit him. But fear of the Outermost Edge of the World spurred him on.

Little by little the thick wall of green thinned, until Yaroslav found himself at the edge of a desert. Shading his eyes against the dazzling sun, he scanned the land and sky long and carefully. But Baba Yaga and the firebird were nowhere to be seen.

The thought of crossing the trackless desert filled him with dread. But his greater dread of the Outermost Edge of the World drove him onward. Day after day, nearly blinded by the sizzling sun, he struggled through an endless sea of sand, sometimes walking but more often crawling.

When at last he reached the other side of the desert, he found himself at the foot of a range of shaggy, snow-covered mountains. But no sign of Baba Yaga or the firebird did he see. "I can't go on," he cried.

Then Yaroslav thought he heard the shrill cackle of Baba Yaga in the sharp winds that swept down from the mountains and whistled about him. "Outermost Edge of the World! Outermost Edge of the World!"

"I'm not beaten yet!" he shouted, shaking his fist at his unseen foe.

Soon he was knee-deep in snow. More snow began to fall. It swirled about him so thickly that often he could not see where he was going. He grew numb with cold. He could not think. He stumbled. He fell. He picked himself up and struggled on, until finally he climbed the last mountain.

Yaroslav gasped at what lay below. Spread out as far as he could see was swampland. He knew that somewhere in that swampland Baba Yaga had a hut that stood on chicken legs. And his heart beat faster at the thought of finding the firebird and avoiding the Outermost Edge of the World.

A short time later Yaroslav was slogging slowly through the oozy swamp. As he looked for Baba Yaga's hut, he tried not to see the alligators and snakes that surrounded him on all sides. The marshy goo gripped his feet so tightly that many times he thought he could not take another step. When vultures circled above him, however, he summoned the strength to go on.

As if in a trance, Yaroslav worked his way across the swampland, seeking, ever seeking, but never finding Baba Yaga's hut. At last he reached the far side of the swamp and slumped to the ground, senseless.

When he awoke, he found himself lying under a pomegranate tree. "Where am I?" he murmured to himself.

He sat up, and his wonder-struck eyes drank in the breath-taking beauty that surrounded him.

Suddenly a familiar cackle aroused Yaroslav from his reverie. "Baba Yaga!" he cried, rolling to his feet to face her.

"Welcome to the Outermost Edge of the World!" she shrieked.

"But I thought—"

"I know what you thought, fool. That's how I got you here."

Then Yaroslav noticed the firebird, perched on the top of the pomegranate tree, preening its golden wings and looking as if it had never left the golden cage. He could see that the firebird no longer needed him—and he knew he no longer needed it.

Yaroslav stayed at the Outermost Edge of the World only long enough to renew body and spirit. Then he made the difficult journey back, now with a lighter heart.

Returning to his kingdom, he reclaimed his throne and made peace with his queen. And thereafter he ruled with such thoughtfulness and understanding that he became known to one and all as Yaroslav the Wise.